W9-AUT-950

Open House
for Butterflies

by
Ruth Krauss

Pictures by
Maurice Sendak

HARPER & ROW, PUBLISHERS

OPEN HOUSE FOR BUTTERFLIES
Text Copyright © 1960 by Ruth Krauss
Pictures Copyright © 1960 by Maurice Sendak
Printed in the United States of America
All rights in this book are reserved.
Library of Congress catalog card number: 60-5782

A screaming song is good to
know in case you need to scream

A good thing to think about is
what kind of face to make when
you say please

If you're a horse
a good thing to
think about is
a castle of sugar lumps

You should make a sad face
when you meet a crocodile

A baby is very convenient to be

Open house for butterflies
is a good thing to have

Look

 Look

Look

Look

Look

Look

Look! I'm running away with my imagination

Lapkin is a good word to know

Nojuice is a good word to know
in case you have a glass of no juice

Dogdog is a good word to know in case you
see a dog and you see it in a looking glass too

I have a two-wheeler

I have a three-wheeler

I have a broken-wheeler

Broken-wheeler is a good word to know

There should be a parade
when a baby is born

A baby is so you
could be the boss

A good way to tell it's snowing is
when everybody runs outside and
throws their hats in the air

The minute you meet some people
you know you will hate their mothers

Lovabye is a good word to know

Suppose
old people
grew down as
young people
grew up

A good way to get yourself to go to bed
is yell **All aboard for bed!**

I always go to bed
after my bedtime

When you're very very tired just
throw your tired away

Pink means nightie

Easter eggs are all different outside
but they're all alike inside

Can a
bride fly?

A wedding song is good to
know in case you're at a wedding

icky goo
icky goo
icky goo
goo goo

A work song for clay is good to know

I made a little
clay ball and
threw it hard
and it got flat
and now I have a flat ball

bump

bump

bumpety

A song for bumpy roads is good to know

A good thing to know is what a punch in
the nose feels like in case somebody asks

Do you want a punch in the nose?

A baby makes the mother
and father—otherwise they're
just plain people

Yesterday shows another day is here

Are you pretending
you're really a lion?

If you're pretending you're a
lion it's good to know if you're
pretending you're really a lion

Remember the day we
went to the city?

No

If you went out and forgot your
pretend friends where would you
go when you went back for them?

–the day we went
to see the tall
buildings–

No

–the day we
went on
the train–

Oh! You mean the
day the
elephant
climbed
the tree

A good thing
to know is this road
is private for everybody

A good thing
not to be is
a plant because someone might think
you are a weed and pull you up by the roots

I wouldn't
want to be
an apple

A queen suit is a good thing
to have in case you're planning
to be a queen when you grow up

A little tree is a good thing not to be because
you might grow up to be a telephone pole

Can a caboose
grow up?

Big shows you grew

Marriage is so your brothers and sisters should grow up and get married and then you could be the only child

Grownup means to go to nursery school

Everybody should be quiet
near a little stream and listen

A bowl of milk is a good thing to take along
in case you're pretending you're a kitten

I like little thunder

One thing no good about a big brother is
when you hit him he hits you right back

Yanh yanh yanh!
I don't have a
little red wagon
and you do

You can always boast you **don't** have it

What would
happen if I
didn't dot
the i?

When you run out
of cereal can you
run into it again?

A good way to make an Indian hat is cut a picket fence out of
paper and put the ends together and you'll have an Indian hat

There are all kinds of ears
in this world

A nose is to be
nosey with

Pins never unfit you
you can wear them your whole life

A baby dances with its feet in the air

If I had a tail I'd pull my wagon
with it while I was picking flowers

If I had a tail
I wouldn't be a lion
I might eat too many
people and then I'd get sick

If I had a tail I'd give it to someone who needs it

I think a race looks
prettier when
everybody comes
in even

A good way to end a story is

The prince and the princess lived happy ever after and the mice lived happy ever after too